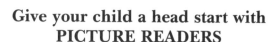

Give your child a head start with
PICTURE READERS

Dear Parent,

Now children as young as preschool age can have the fun and satisfaction of reading a book all on their own.

In every Picture Reader, there are simple words, rebus pictures, and 24 flash cards to cut out and keep. (There is a flash card for every rebus picture plus extra cards for reading practice.) After children listen to each story a couple of times, they will be ready to try it all by themselves.

Collect all the titles in our Picture Reader series. Once children have mastered these books, they can move on to Levels 1, 2, and 3 in our All Aboard Reading series.

ISBN 0-448-41499-6 A B C D E F G H I J

A PICTURE READER

DOT HAS SPOTS

By Roberta Edwards
Illustrated by Bettina Paterson

Grosset & Dunlap • New York

Dot and Lotta

were best friends.

They were making

sand

with their  .

Lotta looked at Dot.

"There is a spot

on your  ."

4

Yes! Dot did have

a spot

on her

and on her

and on her .

She showed her spots

to her mom.

"Oh!" said Mom.

"We must go to

the  NOW!"

The  looked at Dot

and her spots.

"It's pox!"

said the .

Mom and Dot

got in the  .

They went back

to Dot's  .

Mom put Dot

in her  .

Mom put Binky

the

in  too.

Dot felt hot.

Now she had

more spots.

Poor Dot!

Mom gave Dot

some

from a .

Dad read Dot a  .

Soon Dot was asleep.

The next day

Dot felt a little better.

She put on

with red spots.

She put a

in her  .

The had

red spots too.

The next day

Dot played

with Mom.

The red ones

were like red spots.

The next day

Dad brought Dot

with a 🍒 on top.

The 🍒 was like

a red spot too.

Dot saw lots

of red spots—

Mom's ,

a slice of ,

and a on TV.

Then one day

Dot had no more spots.

But guess who did?

Lotta!

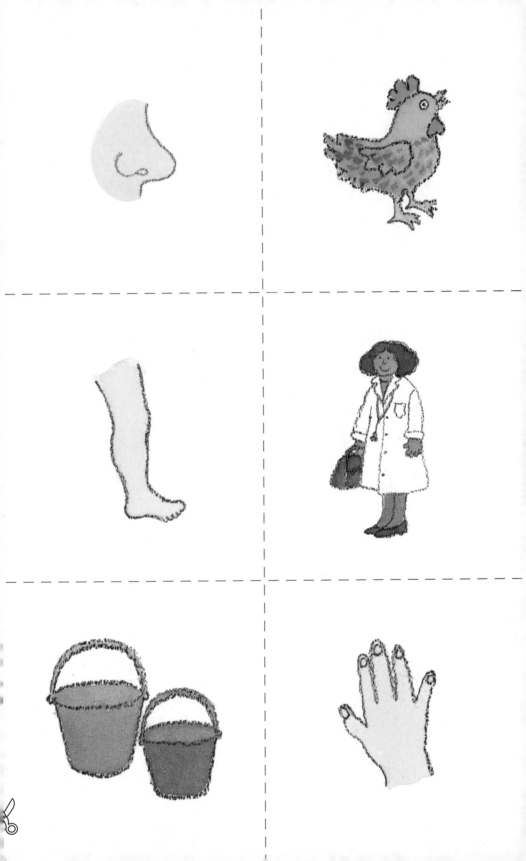

chicken	nose
doctor	leg
hand	pails

cherry	ice cream
bear	bed
bottle	car

checkers	hair
shovels	cakes
frog	house

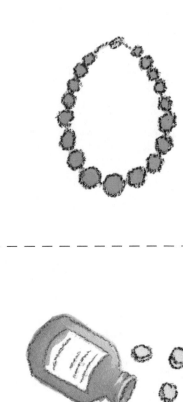
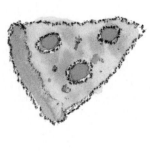

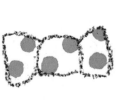

pizza	beads
book	pills
bow	pajamas